Lighthouse Lullaby
by
KELLY PAUL BRIGGS

DOWN EAST BOOKS

ISBN 0-89272-549-4
Library of Congress Catalog Card Number: 2001095191
Book design by Janet L. Patterson
Printed in China

5   4   3   2   1

Down East Books
Rockport, Maine
Book orders: 1-800-766-1670

For my son, Bailey—

Because I love you

"all the way to the moon and back."

4

Snowflakes tumble to the earth,

Slow and silent through the sky.

Lapping waves against the rocks

Sing out a lighthouse lullaby.

6

Island home built snug and true

Where the stone hearth's fire glows.

Mama bakes while Papa leaves

To bring the flock in from the snow.

Velvet noses sniff the air.

The black-faced sheep are coming home.

Shuffle, shuffle eager hooves

Past snowdrift fields and walls of stone.

10

Bells *ding ding* as restless goats

Trip-trot along on rhythmic feet

Up the snaky, snowy path

Past twisted vines of bittersweet.

Gentle Belgian paws the ground

And prances once around his pen

As he awaits his master's hand

To lift the latch and lead him in.

Old brown barn with weathered shingles,

Sheltered by the rugged hills.

Cozy stalls laid thick with straw,

And snow piled on the windowsills.

Lofty spruce with heavy arms

protecting creatures big and small,

Swaying bravely in the dark

while foxes creep and barred owls call.

Lighted by a hazy moon,

A playful snowman all alone

Waves his branch arms in the wind

And wears a smile of shell and stone.

Mittens drying by the fire.

Little fingers, frosty white,

Hold a cup of warm sweet cider.

Island child, sleep well tonight.

Pictures hanging on the walls

Of famous ships and ocean scenes.

Papa hugs his sleepy boy,

Then tucks him in and says, "Sweet dreams."

24

Scents of Mama's just-baked rolls

Are drifting up the open stair.

Underneath her handstitched quilt,

Tired arms embrace a teddy bear.

Papa's high up in the tower,

Standing watch throughout the night.

Guarding precious life below,

He is the keeper of the light.

Sailing ships are passing by,

Bound for ports like Baltimore.

The beacon lamp is burning bright

To steer them from the rocky shore.

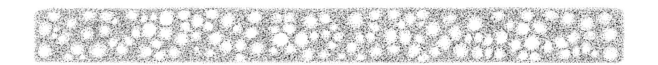

Icy pine boughs tap the window.

Little child, with peaceful sigh,

Drifting slowly off to sleep

Upon a lighthouse lullaby.

Author's Note

Lighthouse Lullaby grew from my interest in the families who tended remote island lighthouses around 1900. I was particularly touched by stories I read about William C. Williams, who was the keeper at dangerous Boon Island Light (off Cape Neddick, Maine) for twenty-six years. While researching his background, I stumbled upon the Williams family photo album at the York Historical Society, and my inspiration for the pictures in this book started there. A nineteenth-century photograph of Boon Island Light from the Shore Village Museum was the model for my lighthouse family's home.

Thank you,

Virginia Spiller, of the York Historical Society;
Wayne Wheeler, Director of the United States Lighthouse Society;
and Robert Davis, at the Shore Village Museum, Rockland, Maine.

And special thanks to my mentor, Baron.